Dedication:

I want to thank Dave Branon, Clarissa Thomasson, and the folks at Piscataqua Press for all the help and encouragement you've given me with *Amos*.

Thomas Rhodes

Amos Booker: One Man's Journey with Jesus
Copyright 2018 by Thomas Rhodes
Printed in the USA by
Piscataqua Press
32 Daniel St.
Portsmouth, NH
03801

ISBN: 978-1-944393-93-9

www.piscataquapress.com

CHAPTER ONE

Amos Booker was called by God when he was a little boy. He grew up in the heart of the Mississippi Delta, and he loved fishing and playing outside with his brothers and sisters in the hot sun. Being the youngest meant that Amos had to fight for his share at the dinner table—that is when there was dinner. Those times when he got sick and scared, his momma was there to hold him and tell him that God loved him and that everything was going to be all right. And she made him memorize John 3:16: "For God so loved the world that He gave his only begotten Son, that whoever believes in Him should not perish, but have everlasting life." She helped Amos understand that all people are sinners in need of a Savior and that Savior is Jesus, who died and shed His blood on the cross for the sins of mankind. Amos Booker was seven years old when he received Jesus as his Lord and Savior.

Six months later, Momma died, and Amos and his brothers and sisters were split up and scattered. Some went to live with relatives, and others, Amos included, were sent to an orphanage in Louisiana called the "Heavenly Angels Orphanage." It was anything but "heavenly." The children were beaten regularly; the food wasn't fit for dogs; and there was no education to speak of. Those children who tried to escape never got further than the surrounding swamps, and some were never seen again.

Momma had given Amos a pocket New Testament for his birthday. Amazingly, the orphanage had not discovered it. One night as Amos was lying on his dirty mattress and listening to the cries and bad dreams of the other children he remembered another verse of scripture he'd memorized from the book of Matthew, where God says: "Do not fear therefore; you are of more value than many sparrows." With this message of comfort, Amos finally fell asleep.

Amos Booker was ten years old when he was adopted out of the Heavenly Angels Orphanage. One of his brothers had drowned in the swamps while trying to escape the orphanage; and a sister had died from "complications" from pneumonia. But Amos was still looking to God for deliverance. It came on a day he least expected it. He was being led to what they called the "Punishment Room" because he had been caught teaching the other children how to pray at mealtime. This did not set well with the head of the orphanage, a very large and very angry man named Master Roland. Master Roland didn't want anything or anyone—including God—getting in the way of total obedience to him and his supervisors. Thanking God for food was not going to happen at the Heavenly Angels Orphanage.

Isaiah and Charlene West were childless and wanted a child. Isaiah was a cook, and Charlene a seamstress, and they both loved Jesus. They lived and worked near the orphanage, and they prayed for the children there all the time. Master Roland and his evil ways were well-known in the area, and it was thought that the man had political connections. It was on the very day that ten-year-old Amos Booker was being taken to the Punishment Room that Isaiah and Charlene West decided to come to the Heavenly Angels Orphanage to adopt a child.

As they sat in the interview room with Master Roland and his supervisors, they were told about a young boy named Amos, who was a "troublemaker." Isaiah and Charlene just looked at each other and started smiling and laughing. "Praise God, we're about to have a son. Thank you, Jesus!"

CHAPTER TWO

Isaiah and Charlene West knew they had to be very patient with their new son, ten-year-old Amos Booker. He'd been through a lot in his three-year stay at the Heavenly Angels Orphanage. Two of his siblings had died; he was malnourished; and he sometimes had trouble sleeping at night—remembering the cries and bad dreams of the other children at the orphanage. But slowly—and with the help of God—Amos, Isaiah, and Charlene became a family.

Charlene especially understood the needs of a little boy who'd lost his mother at such a young age. Amos got a whole lot of loving from this woman—hugs, kisses, and plenty of good food. She knew that soon Amos would be enrolled at the local school in their area and that it wouldn't be easy for him. But she also knew there was something special about this child. She'd sensed it when she saw him clutching his New Testament close when they brought him home from the orphanage. Yes, she thought, God has big plans for this little boy—big plans.

There was still one month to go before school would begin, so Amos got a chance to get to know his new parents better. Some days Isaiah would bring him to the restaurant where he was a cook: Kingsford's House of Ribs. Everyone there loved the man. He could put a smile on anyone's face. And when they found out he had a new son, well, they just had to see the boy. That's how Amos ended up with a whole bunch of new friends. He loved watching Isaiah cook up all those good dishes, and he loved watching how all the restaurant workers worked together to make good things happen for the customers. Seeing the smiles, the laughter, and everybody having a good time, was a very special time for the young Amos Booker.

Sunday mornings the West family attended church at Rock of Ages Bible Church a few miles down the road from where they lived. The preacher there was an old man named Reverend Waters. He'd been preaching the Word of God at this church since before Isaiah and Charlene were born, and he was still going strong. He just loved opening the Bible and telling people about Jesus.

The first thing Reverend Waters did when he met ten-year-old Amos Booker was to lift him high up in the air and tell him how glad he was to meet him. Amos wasn't scared at all. He knew right away that this man was a close friend of God's. Isaiah and Charlene were both surprised at how quickly the old preacher and their young son hit it off. Their little "troublemaker" was turning out to be a real blessing in their lives.

Charlene walked with Amos to his first day at school. She could feel his small hand shaking in hers as they neared the school, and she stopped and leaned down to talk to him. She reminded Amos how God had protected him at the Heavenly Angels Orphanage and said that He would protect him now. Her new son just smiled up at her. He wasn't afraid. He was excited, and he kissed her and broke away from her and ran toward to school for his first day.

Once again Charlene West found herself in awe of God, and of a special little boy named Amos Booker. She knew that Isaiah was going to enjoy hearing about this. Charlene walked back to her home with a song in her heart and a very big smile on her face.

CHAPTER THREE

The next few years went by as quick as a flash of lightning in a storm for the West family. Charlene was still doing her seamstress work, and Isaiah had been promoted to manager at Kingsford's House of Ribs. Amos Booker was now a tall, gangly teenager who loved listening to gospel music—especially the "Blind Boys of Alabama."

His early school years had started out rough because in the beginning there was this mean, nasty young boy named Early Baker, who loved picking on the weaker kids at recess. One day, Early was kicking and punching another boy in the schoolyard while all the other kids just stood there and watched—except Amos! He ran to the fight, jumped in the middle of it and started praying. Early was shocked. He didn't know what to do. But all of a sudden, he found himself calming down and looking at this new kid, Amos Booker.

By then the teacher, Miss June, had come outside to see what was going on, although she already knew—it had to be Early. Instead of chaos in the schoolyard, she saw peace. Miss June had been asking the Lord to get a hold of Early Baker, and this quiet schoolyard was the answer to her prayer.

Amos and Early became best friends. They went fishing together, and in the summer when school was out, Isaiah West gave them both jobs in the kitchen at Kingsford's House of Ribs. At first, Early didn't want any part of going to Sunday school with Amos. His momma and daddy both drank a lot and cursed and everything, and Early was afraid of getting whipped for hanging out with religious folks.

All that changed one day when Early's parents got a knock on their door. It was the Reverend Waters from the Rock of Ages Bible Church. He shook their hands warmly, smiled, and asked their permission for Early to be able to come to Sunday school with his best friend, Amos Booker. Then something amazing happened. Joe and Betty Baker grabbed a hold of the old preacher's sleeve, thanked him, and said yes. Early could go. Reverend Waters walked back down the country road towards his church laughing and thanking God. Ever since young Amos Booker had become a part of Isaiah and Charlene's family, lots of good things were happening in people's lives—including his. Thank You, Lord, for Amos.

Amos was twenty-four-years old when Reverend Waters died. God had given the old preacher fifty-one years of service, and the church was filled with folks who'd been touched by his godly life. Amos's daddy, Isaiah, was one of the speakers at the memorial service. And Amos found out for the first time how the Reverend

Waters had literally plucked seventeen-year-old Isaiah West out of a local street gang and placed him in a Sunday school class taught by his younger sister, Miss Margie.

All of Isaiah's street smarts were no match for the loving but tough Miss Margie. She was down on her knees day and night praying for the young man's soul. And in Sunday school the Holy spirit helped Miss Margie make the Bible come alive for Isaiah and the others in the class. It was here that Isaiah West met and fell in love with the woman of his dreams, Charlene Royce. Yes, the Reverend Waters' legacy of love through Christ had touched many lives.

The service ended with the singing of the hymn "Amazing Grace," and now it was time to head on over to the House of Ribs for a celebration of Reverend Waters' home-going. It was a sad but joyous day.

CHAPTER FOUR

The congregation at Rock of Ages Bible Church had a huge decision to make: who was the Lord calling to be their new preacher? Three generations of church members had grown up and worshipped with Reverend Waters—and now he was gone. Who would stand in the pulpit and lead the flock? Who would exhort them to stand strong in the Word of God? This was a serious matter, so the first thing the church elders did was to call a mid-week prayer meeting—at which time they all got down on their faces before God and beseeched Him for wisdom and guidance in this matter.

A half hour went by, then an hour, and then one of the worshippers got up and went over to the church piano and started playing hymns of praise. Then everyone stood up and began singing and clapping and praising the Lord as the elders shouted out promises from the scriptures. The Spirit was leading, and soon the Rock of Ages Bible Church would have its new preacher.

Early Baker was still best friends with Amos Booker. His life, too, had been touched by the Reverend Waters. A few years after his conversion to Christ, he'd signed up for the military with his parents' blessing. Joe and Betty

Baker were starting to get interested in this whole gospel thing—especially after seeing the change in their son, Early. They knew that no earthly power could have gotten a hold of Early and changed him like that. It had to be God. So they got real curious.

While Early was still in basic training, they began listening to Christian programs on the radio. They still weren't ready to visit Rock of Ages Bible Church. They knew that Reverend Waters had passed and that the church was looking for a new preacher. Maybe when that happened, they'd come by for a visit. In the meantime, Joe and Betty were learning more about their son's faith through Christian radio. Slowly, but surely, God was calling.

The elders and deacons presented their choice for the new preacher to the congregation at Rock of Ages. They'd sought out the Lord with fasting and prayer, and now they had their man: Amos Booker. And the folks at church agreed. Even though Amos had no formal seminary training, he'd sat under the godly teaching of both Reverend Waters and his sister, Miss Margie, for years. He was a keen student of the scriptures, and he knew how to take the word of God and share it in everyday language. But most of all, Amos Booker loved the Lord deeply, and over the years he'd put that love into action: running the church's food pantry, visiting the prisoners in jail and the sick at the hospital, and doing many other good works for Christ. The Lord had revealed Himself to Amos when he was seven-years-old, and now

He was calling him to shepherd the flock at Rock of Ages Bible Church. Another chapter was about to begin in Amos Booker's life, and many lives were going to be impacted.

Isaiah and Charlene West were having a quiet supper at home when the call came from the elders at church. Charlene took the call, and she started dancing around the kitchen and praising God. Her son, Amos, was going to be the new preacher at Rock of Ages. She put Isaiah on the phone, and then he began shouting and dancing with Charlene around the kitchen. Their prayers had been answered. What a privilege and responsibility Amos would now have: stepping into the pulpit for the godly Reverend Waters and leading the congregation at church.

Isaiah was already planning a celebration of this event at Kingsford's House of Ribs, and he and Charlene couldn't wait to tell their son the good news. And then they got another call that night that would sorely test the faith of everyone involved: Early Baker was dead.

CHAPTER FIVE

A mos was leading a Bible study at the home of a church member when Isaiah and Charlene called. He was about to experience a moment from the hand of God that no human wisdom could explain. Charlene asked to speak to Amos. She told him that he was now the new preacher at Rock of Ages Bible Church. And then she broke down, and Isaiah got on the phone. He told his son that Early Baker was dead—having been killed in a car crash near his military base.

Amos dropped the phone, and his legs buckled under him. Another Bible study member got on the phone with Isaiah, while the others knelt down on the floor, laid their hands on Amos, and began praying. They knew that something was terribly wrong and that their friend and brother needed their comfort and prayers—and needed them now.

Amos Booker's first official duty as the new preacher at Rock of Ages was presiding over the memorial service for his best friend, Early Baker. The church was filled to overflowing for a young man whose life had been totally transformed by God. A little boy who was a schoolyard bully had grown up to be a devout follower of Christ.

Amos was still grieving for his friend, and yet he knew he was in a better place, and that was the message he would preach at this service: the good news of the Bible.

There were two people not at Early's service: his parents, Joe and Betty Baker. When they got the news about their son, Joe picked up the radio he'd used to listen to Christian programs and smashed it against the wall. Then he stormed out of the house and went off on a seven-day drinking binge. When the police finally found Joe, he was lying under a bridge covered in vomit and smelling of whiskey. They took him to the ER at the VA hospital.

Betty Baker sat there alone in an empty house for a week—barely eating or sleeping, just staring off into space and then rocking back and forth in grief. Her baby was gone, and that was that. Where were you, God, she thought. Where were You?

Isaiah West was concerned about his wife, Charlene. Even before they'd gotten the good news about Amos being named the new preacher at Rock of Ages Bible Church, Isaiah had noticed that Charlene was looking tired—Real Tired! When he mentioned to Charlene that she'd missed her annual checkup, she just laughed it off and said she was feeling fine. Until one night at supper when she got dizzy and short of breath, and Isaiah wouldn't take no for an answer. They were going to the ER to have her looked at.

Isaiah paced back and forth in the waiting room, wanting to rely on God but scared of what he thought he might hear from the doctor. Outside of his momma, Charlene was the only woman he'd ever loved. They'd had a lot of good years together, and Isaiah wasn't ready to let go of his dear wife."Please, God, don't take her now. Amos and me, we need her. Please don't take her now." And then the doctor came out of the ER and walked toward Isaiah West.

Charlene West had had a mild heart attack. She was going to need rest—and lots of it—and nursing care as she recovered her strength. Isaiah and Amos sought the Lord in prayer about this because nursing care would cost a lot, and the Wests were not rich people. Amos's preacher salary wouldn't be enough, and he didn't want to burden the folks at church. Then somebody remembered that Early Baker's momma, Betty, used to be a nurse before the drinking got to her. Amos Booker knew that now was the time he needed to be paying a visit to his best friend's momma, Betty Baker.

CHAPTER SIX

Betty Baker was still getting over the loss of her son, Early. She was hurting bad, not eating right and hardly sleeping at all. The only good news was that she hadn't had a drink in weeks. Somehow she sensed that more drinking would only dishonor her son's memory. But her husband, Joe, was still wrestling with the bottle. The VA was there to help him, but he just couldn't accept Early's death. He left the house each day with a full bottle of whiskey and returned home at night when it was empty. Betty couldn't go on like this: grieving over Early and watching Joe destroy himself. And then one day when Joe was out of the house, she found herself silently asking God to show her a way out of this. There was a knock on the door, and standing there was her son's best friend, the Reverend Amos Booker, the new preacher at Rock of Ages Bible Church.

Amos hadn't seen Betty Baker since before Early's death. They both just stood there for a moment. Words weren't needed. Then they hugged, and Betty wept on Amos's shoulder. He felt her pain keenly. This had to be the Lord's timing for deliverance for this woman, he thought. They sat at the kitchen table and drank coffee and shared memories of Early.

After a few minutes, Betty was even laughing as she told Amos about the time Early got a pass from his base to come home and surprise her and Joe on their wedding anniversary. And they both laughed when Amos told Betty about the time when he and Early trapped a large, old turtle and turned it loose in the church sanctuary— just as Reverend Waters was getting ready to preach a Sunday morning sermon. The old preacher turned the tables on them by picking up the turtle, carrying it up behind the pulpit and proclaiming: "This old turtle and me, we've seen a lot of change. But one thing you can count on that's never going to change, the gospel of Jesus Christ." The congregation all stood up and applauded, and Amos and Early were laughing and applauding, too.

As Amos and Betty finished their coffee, the young preacher got to his point. His momma, Charlene, was pretty sick and in need of some good nursing care. Amos took a deep breath and then asked Betty Baker if she'd be willing to help out for a small salary. Betty sat there for a minute—not knowing whether to laugh or cry. Then she said one simple word: "Yes."

Joe Baker was furious when Betty told him she was going to be looking after Charlene West. He was blaming all those "Holy Rollers" for Early's death. If he and Betty hadn't listened to Reverend Waters and let their boy go to Sunday school with Amos Booker, then Early wouldn't have gotten all caught up with that religious stuff. He would have stayed home and not gone into the service and not gotten killed in the car crash. Somewhere inside, Joe knew this wasn't right thinking. This was the booze talking. And he knew what a lousy dad he'd been to Early.

That first morning after Betty went off to take care of Charlene West, Joe sat there at the kitchen table staring at the bottle of whiskey in front of him. Then, without even knowing how it happened, he found himself talking to God—talking about stuff he'd never shared with his wife or son. A few minutes later, Joe Baker did something he'd been taught a man never did—he cried. He cried for Early. He cried for Betty and all the misery he'd caused her over the years. And he asked God for another chance to hear the good news of the Gospel after he'd sobered up. Then Joe stood up from the kitchen table, took the bottle of whiskey and poured it down the kitchen sink. It was time to get serious about his drinking problem. It was time to call the VA.

CHAPTER SEVEN

Isaiah West and Amos Booker were real glad to see Betty Baker that first day she came to look after Charlene. They put out some coffee and cookies for her just to make her feel welcome. Charlene was glad to see Betty, too, but she was a little anxious about the whole thing. All her life—first as a young Charlene Royce and then later on as Mrs. Charlene West—she'd been the one reaching out to others and always lending a helping hand. It was in her nature to be that way, but when the Lord got a hold of her and saved her, the whole giving thing became more joyful. Now Charlene wasn't just giving because it made her feel good; she was giving out of a real love for Jesus. And here she was laid up in bed for awhile on doctor's orders, unable to do anything for Isaiah or Amos or anyone at church. Not only that, but now Charlene had to get used to being cared for by a woman she really didn't know all that well, Betty Baker. Charlene West had spent her whole life giving, and now the Lord had another lesson for her to learn: a lesson on receiving. And Betty was going to be a big part of that lesson.

Amos Booker was getting settled in as the new

preacher at Rock of Ages Bible Church. He continued visiting the prisoners in jail and the sick at the local hospital. The busy chaplains there were always glad for Amos's help. And just like Reverend Waters, Amos loved opening the Bible and telling people about Jesus. Those times when the collection plate was light, he was grateful for the part-time work his daddy, Isaiah, had for him at Kingsford's House of Ribs. After all, he remembered, Saint Paul had been a tentmaker.

Amos was also grateful that his momma, Charlene, was getting better and becoming good friends with Betty Baker and that Joe Baker was getting help for his drinking problem at the VA. Life was good in the community and at church, but soon the Lord would have another test of faith for the Reverend Amos Booker, and once again everyone at Rock of Ages would be called upon to access the Throne of Grace in prayer.

CHAPTER EIGHT

Although Amos and his flock at church had continued to pray for the children at the Heavenly Angels Orphanage, Amos himself had not returned to the orphanage for a visit since his adoption by Isaiah and Charlene fifteen years earlier. They never spoke to him about it. They believed that in God's timing their son would in some way have dealings with the orphanage in the future, but that would be between the Lord and Amos. So they kept that to themselves in prayer.

In the meantime, Charlene and Betty were getting along just fine. Berry had gotten used to watching daytime television in the old days when Joe was at his construction job and Early was at school because she worked the night shift at the hospital and her days were pretty empty. But now as she was looking after Charlene, she had a chance to talk to another woman around her own age about things the men folk don't usually get into. And gradually, as their friendship grew, Betty found herself more at ease talking to Charlene about spiritual things, especially the Christian faith that Early had embraced before his death. Betty Baker was coming ever closer to the Kingdom of God.

Amos Booker got an urgent call just before the Sunday morning service was due to begin at church. It was from the Salvation Army homeless shelter just north of the Heavenly Angels Orphanage. A little nine-year-old boy named Jonas had managed to escape from the orphanage, and he was in pretty bad shape. The homeless shelter was already overcrowded with men— most of them rough around the edges. Was there any way that the Reverend Booker and the folks at Rock of Ages Bible Church might be able to help this little boy?

Amos Booker suddenly felt a cold, hard anger come upon him as he struggled to control his emotions— thinking not only of nine-year-old Jonas but also flashing back to a scared little seven-year-old boy named Amos walking through the large, old gates of an orphanage in the heart of Louisiana swamp country. After telling the Salvation Army he was on his way, Amos turned over his sermon to one of the elders and broke the speed limit as he raced to pick up a child who was in desperate need of help—as he once was. And there was something else that Amos Booker knew that God was placing upon his heart: the Heavenly Angels Orphanage and the man who was still running it after all these years, Master Roland. This man was most worthy of a day of reckoning, even as he was in need of salvation. But first, there was the matter of little Jonas. "Oh, Lord, show me the way" prayed Amos. "Show me the way!"

The first thing Amos saw when he walked into the waiting room at the homeless shelter was a skinny little boy sitting alone in a corner of the room, looking off into space. As he got closer, Amos could see that Jonas had some black and blue marks on him—as well as bug bites from the swamps. He was covered in a light blanket and shivering, but not from any cool weather. Amos Booker felt his anger rising again. How in the world did this child get away from those monsters at the orphanage? But then he realized immediately. It was the Lord who'd delivered Jonas safely to the Salvation Army and now to his care. "Thank You, Jesus. Thank You."

CHAPTER NINE

Joe Baker was starting to feel better. The VA treatment program was helping. Neither one of his parents had been heavy drinkers, but Joe had started down that path when he was in the service. He saw combat and a lot of things he wanted to forget, so he and his army buddies drank. They drank a lot.

Joe had known Betty Smith since high school, but they'd never dated. It wasn't until he got out of the service and came back home that he asked her out. Betty was a shy, quiet young woman, and she sensed an element of excitement and even a little danger in Joe that unnerved and intrigued her at the same time. Her girlfriends and her head said "no," but her heart said "yes."

Their first date was at the Strand Theater downtown. Afterwards, Joe took Betty for a burger, fries, and a milkshake, and he sat there and listened as she brought him up to date on the latest news in town. She confessed that she might have thought about him once or twice in high school. She'd been a sophomore when Joe went into the service, and they'd both done some growing up since then. Betty was now in nursing school, and Joe had a construction job lined up with his uncle. Six months later, Betty Smith became Betty Baker, and a year later, they had Early.

Joe Baker sat in the sun room at the VA—remembering a young and beautiful Betty Smith and a happy, healthy baby boy named Early. He wanted another chance with his wife. And Joe Baker wanted another child—if God was willing.

Isaiah West had so much to be thankful for. His beloved wife, Charlene, was getting better, and through her love and friendship, her friend and caretaker, Betty Baker, had heard the message of salvation and put her faith in Jesus Christ. His son, Amos Booker, had just completed his first year of preaching at the Rock of Ages Bible Church. Isaiah knew how proud old Reverend Waters would be of Amos, and especially of how Amos had responded during the time of Early Baker's death and then Charlene's illness—being tested in the fire of God's refining process and coming through it stronger.

Isaiah was also thankful for being promoted to manager at Kingsford's House of Ribs. The owner, Mr. Al Kingsford, was a faithful man of God who saw his restaurant as a ministry, and he counted on Isaiah West (through the Spirit) to keep that joyful atmosphere going at the House of Ribs.

Now another time of testing had come upon Isaiah's son, Amos, as there was another little orphan boy named Jonas in need of help. God had sent him into the loving arms of the Rock of Ages Bible Church and the Reverend

Amos Booker. Isaiah West knew that with the Lord everything was going to turn out all right.

CHAPTER TEN

Soon after their marriage, God had blessed Isaiah and Charlene with a nice-sized three-bedroom home; and over the years, many out-of-town relatives and friends had come to visit. This home had been the center of many happy get-togethers and meals for God's people—a real ministry of hospitality. Amos had grown to manhood here. Charlene had been restored to good health here. Now there would be another special guest in the West's happy home: nine-year-old Jonas Armstrong.

At first, Isaiah was concerned that having Jonas in their home so soon after Charlene's recovery might be a strain on her. But they both felt a peace about it after praying. They sensed that this would only be a temporary situation, and that the Lord had already picked out a future home for the boy. It was just a matter of time. Since Amos now had his own living accommodations at the church parsonage, there would also be times when Jonas could spend a couple of days a week with the Reverend Booker. Helping Jonas Armstrong back to good health would be God's latest project for the congregation at Rock of Ages Bible

Church, and it would remind them all of their total dependence upon the Lord.

Jonas came to spend a couple of days with Amos after he'd been at the West's for about a month. Charlene had tried to mother the little boy—as she'd done with Amos—with lots of hugs and kisses and good food. But Jonas resisted her affection and hardly ate his food, and he wouldn't talk about his past life before his time at the Heavenly Angels Orphanage.

Isaiah and Charlene already knew of the horrors he'd experienced under Master Roland and his supervisors, but his previous history was a question mark. All they knew was that this little nine-year-old was coming from a different place than their son. But they also knew that it was the same loving God that had sent both boys to them. They knew that whatever was troubling Jonas Armstrong, the Lord would provide just the right kind of help and healing in His own time. Their ministry right now was to show Jonas the love of Christ and to lift him up in prayer. And their son, Amos, would once again find himself going back to school with Jesus.

CHAPTER ELEVEN

Joe Baker had been sober now for ten months, and he was feeling good. The congregation at Rock of Ages had been praying for him—along with his wife, Betty, who was a brand-new Christian. His muddled thinking was starting to leave him, and for the first time in a long time Joe was looking forward to the future. He still hadn't responded to the Gospel, but he was no longer hostile to those "holy rollers" either.

Joe's favorite drink of choice now was Maxwell House coffee. There were no longer any loud fights with Betty. Joe Baker was no fool. He could see the change in his wife since she'd accepted Christ, the peace she seemed to have. Joe wanted that peace, too, but he still found himself resisting a total surrender to God. He hadn't yet talked to Betty about maybe having more children; they were still young enough. But Joe Baker knew that he needed more time on the wagon before he had that conversation, and so he sat there in his kitchen and poured himself another cup of Maxwell House.

Jonas Armstrong had healed up physically by the time he went to spend a couple of days with Amos Booker, but the young preacher knew that this little boy was still hurting on the inside. No one—not Isaiah or Charlene or anyone else at church—had told Jonas that the Reverend Booker, who came to get him at the Salvation Army, had also once been an orphan at the Heavenly Angels Orphanage. Everybody agreed that the first course of business was to get this nine-year-old used to his new surroundings.

Jonas had been with Isaiah and Charlene West now for a couple of months, and he'd already had a couple of visits with Amos at the church parsonage. Was now the time, thought Amos—as he sat there sharing cookies and hot chocolate with Jonas in the parsonage living room. Both of them sat there quietly for a few minutes enjoying their snack.

Then Amos got up from his chair, went to another room and came back with a picture. He took the picture over to where Jonas was sitting and sat down beside him. Then he showed the picture to Jonas. It was a picture of a large group of little boys sitting in front of a big, old building. There was a long, wide sign on top of the building that read: Heavenly Angels Orphanage. As Jonas looked at the picture, his eyes widened with fear, and he tried to jump up from his chair. Amos gently held Jonas and pointed to the picture. "You see that little boy, right there in the middle of the first row? That was me."

Suddenly, Jonas Armstrong stopped struggling, looked up at Amos Booker and burst into tears. Amos just held Jonas and let the nine-year-old cry it out. God's healing process had begun.

CHAPTER TWELVE

Mandy Johnson was enjoying her new job as a waitress at Kingsford's House of Ribs. She was a niece of the owner, Mr. Al Kingsford, and she, too, was a devout Christian. She'd been happily married in her native Alabama to a wonderful young man, Wesley Johnson, when tragedy struck in the form of cancer. Wesley was only twenty-nine when he passed, and Al Kingsford knew that what his niece needed right now was a change of scenery.

Mandy agreed, and so she'd come to live with her widowed uncle in his large, comfortable home near the restaurant. She'd always been an active young woman, and now she especially needed to be busy after losing Wesley. With a waitress opening at the House of Ribs, she was ready to go to work. It didn't take long for her to feel right at home at the restaurant, and her new manager, Isaiah West, immediately took her under his wing and made her feel right at home.

Mandy was a quick learner, and soon she'd become a customer favorite with her warm smile and friendly ways. And just as all the House of Ribs employees had come to love their new cook, Isaiah, years before, they now felt the same love for Mandy Johnson. Only a few people knew how much she was still hurting, but day by day she bravely kept on. Everyone at Rock of Ages continued to lift Mandy up in prayer, and the Lord heard their prayers. In His perfect timing, He would have a special blessing in store for Miss Mandy Johnson.

Every year toward the end of summer, Mr. Al Kingsford and his House of Ribs restaurant would sponsor a community picnic and barbecue on the village green across from the town hall. All the ladies would bring their delicious side dishes to go along with Mr. Al's famous barbecue beef, chicken, and pork. Large picnic tables were spread out on the grounds and covered with festive tablecloths. Along with the side dishes were biscuits, corn bread, sweet tea, lemonade, sodas and desserts galore: pies, cakes, cobblers, ice cream and so on. No one ever went hungry at this annual feast. It was a great time for families and friends to get together before the kids went back to school—a time for catching up, sharing the good news and the bad news, and –yes— praying for one another. This little Louisiana community was well aware of God's kindness in sickness and in health, and their town motto was: Give Thanks!

Though no one knew it yet, this year's picnic was going to be special for a number of people. Some blessings would be coming their way from the Lord, who according to the Scriptures enjoyed attending social events. And why not the House of Ribs community barbecue and picnic?

CHAPTER THIRTEEN

There were hundreds and hundreds of people at the picnic and Mr. Al's entire restaurant staff including Mandy Johnson. All the church folks from Rock of Ages Bible Church and other churches in the area, and many other townsfolk and business people from the community attended. Everyone was there and ready to have a good time. The master of ceremonies—as always—was Al Kingsford. He loved presiding over this annual gathering, and once again he made ready to open the event with prayer. This year there was a special guest at the picnic: nine-year-old Jonas Armstrong. He'd been coming along well since his time with the Reverend Booker at the parsonage, and now as Mr. Al called Jonas up to the microphone, he came willingly and even allowed himself to be hugged. As always, this year everyone at the picnic lifted up the orphans at the Heavenly Angels Orphanage in prayer—asking His protection over them and thanking the Lord for sending Jonas to them. They also prayed for Master Roland and his supervisors. Amen. Amen.

Amos Booker was glad to be at the community barbecue and picnic as just one of the townsfolk and not wearing his preacher suit. It was so good to be able to come to this gathering and to relax and have fun with family and friends. Amos sat at one of the picnic tables with Isaiah and Charlene, Jonas Armstrong, Joe and Betty Baker, and Mr. Al Kingsford and his niece, Miss Mandy Johnson.

Amos was well-aware of Mandy's loss of her husband, Wesley Johnson, and he and the others at church had been praying for her peace and comfort in the Lord. He'd also been waited on by Mandy at the House of Ribs and had enjoyed some casual conversation with her. One thought continued to run through Amos's mind: this was a godly woman. As he took another bite of his barbecue beef and potato salad, he looked up and saw that Miss Mandy was smiling at him from across the picnic table. Her uncle Al noticed it. Isaiah and Charlene West noticed it. Joe and Betty Baker noticed it. Even little Jonas Armstrong noticed it. All of a sudden, everyone burst out laughing and got down to some real good eating at Mr. Al Kingsford's community barbecue and picnic.

CHAPTER FOURTEEN

Master Roland was losing his grip on the Heavenly Angels Orphanage and on himself. He'd been recently diagnosed with early-onset dementia, but he hadn't told anyone—not his family, not his supervisors, not anyone. He was normally an angry man, but now his anger was exploding continually at the orphanage, and he was coming down hard on everyone there—employees and children alike.

Finally, one of his newer supervisors had had enough. Eddie Carlisle was a recent college graduate with a genuine love for kids—especially those who'd had a rough life. It didn't take him long to figure out that the stories he'd heard about Master Roland and the other supervisors at Heavenly Angels Orphanage were not only true, but even worse than he'd imagined. Eddie knew that speaking up about the horrors at the orphanage could cost him his job, or worse. But the well-being of these children was at stake here, and Eddie wasn't going to let them down. A time of deliverance was at hand at the Heavenly Angels Orphanage, and Eddie Carlisle was going to be a big part of it.

It was now campaign time in Louisiana, and

Kingsford's House of Ribs was about to get a very special visitor, the governor himself. Governor Jules Francois knew he was in a tough race this time around. His opponent was up by three points as election -day neared, and so Francois was visiting every little town and parish he could as quickly as he could, because time was running out.

When Al Kingsford and Isaiah heard that the governor and his people would be coming to their little town, they immediately extended an invitation to these important folks to have a meet-and-greet with the local townsfolk at the House of Ribs. Jules Francois was not only a clever politician, he was also a huge barbecue beef fan, and he'd heard about Kingsford's restaurant for years. Now he was going to have a chance to sample some awesome beef barbecue along with a little down-home politicking.

Al Kingsford, Isaiah West, Mandy Johnson, and the rest of the House of Ribs staff were thrilled and excited when they got the governor's reply: "Mrs. Francois and I thank you for your kind invitation. We accept. My staff people will set up with you the time of our visit. Cordially, Governor Jules Francois."

Already Mr. Al Kingsford was envisioning a new picture he'd be displaying soon in the restaurant: a picture of him shaking hands with the governor of Louisiana. But, keep me humble, Lord, he thought.

CHAPTER FIFTEEN

Jonas Armstrong and Amos Booker had developed a close friendship over the past year. Ten-year-old Jonas was healing up well from his orphanage experience, and he was starting to share little bits and pieces of his earlier life with the Reverend Booker. His momma had abandoned Jonas and his younger sister early on, leaving them in the hands of an abusive, dope-dealing father who enjoyed causing pain. Now Amos had a better understanding of the little boy's suffering, even before his days at the Heavenly Angels Orphanage, and it grieved him. But now Jonas Armstrong was thriving under the care of a loving community and the kindly folks at Rock of Ages Bible Church, and his future was looking bright.

Isaiah and Charlene West knew that the time was getting close for them to be saying goodbye to Jonas. He'd been staying now with them for almost a year, and he was growing into a strong and healthy little boy. The Wests had known all along that Jonas's stay with them would be temporary, and now the Lord was impressing upon them that He had a new family for the ten-year-old to be a part of: the Baker family—Joe and Betty. The congregation at church had been praying about this as well, and they were of the same mind as Isaiah and Charlene—that Joe and Betty were the ones God was calling to be parents to Jonas Armstrong.

While all this was going on, Joe and Betty had been spending time talking about the possibility of having more children. Joe had been sober for over a year now and was back working construction. And Betty had regained her nursing certificate, and she was doing some private nursing care with the elderly. As they both sat there in their house discussing these things, the same idea came to them at the same time: that little Armstrong boy from the orphanage had no permanent home yet, and they had a lot of love to give. Maybe they could talk with Isaiah and Charlene West about this, and then the boy himself. Somehow Joe and Betty Baker knew that their beloved son, Early, would be well pleased with this latest turn of events.

CHAPTER SIXTEEN

Eddie Carlisle, the young supervisor at the Heavenly Angels Orphanage, knew that a miracle had just happened. He had a cousin who worked in a government office at the state capitol who shared his passion for the well-being of orphan kids. Eddie had sent her a private message to be relayed to Governor Jules Francois, in which he revealed his position at the orphanage and asked for a meeting with Francois. Somehow Eddie's cousin had been able to get this message to the governor quietly and under the radar. And now she was calling Eddie Carlisle with the news that Jules Francois and his wife, Helene, were going to be visiting a little town not far from the orphanage the following week—at a place called Kingsford's House of Ribs. The governor had personally assured Eddie's cousin that he and his wife would take the time to sit down with him for a few minutes to hear what he had to say.

Eddie thanked his cousin, and then he thanked the Lord for this amazing turn of events. He was actually going to have a chance to talk with the governor of Louisiana about the out-of-control Master Roland and his abusive supervisors. The time of reckoning was close at hand.

Al Kingsford could see that his niece, Mandy Johnson, was growing fonder and fonder of the Reverend Amos Booker. When she'd first come to live with him, he hadn't said anything to her about the godly young preacher because he knew how much she was still hurting from the loss of her husband, Wesley. But Al did have a secret hope in his heart that in God's good time his precious niece and Amos Booker would take notice of each other. And that day at the picnic when he'd seen Mandy smiling at Amos across the picnic table was a real good day. He knew that his prayers for her were being answered and that her time of mourning had ended. And that now she was getting ready to start a new life, and why not a new life with Amos Booker? Why not?

CHAPTER SEVENTEEN

Joe Baker had invited Jonas Armstrong to go fishing with him, and Jonas had said "yes." So bright and early one morning, Joe picked up the ten-year-old, and they went to one of Joe's favorite spots—where Joe figured they'd have no problem catching a mess of fish. They just sat there for a while in silence, waiting for a bite on their lines. Jonas Armstrong knew that this was more than a fishing trip with Mr. Baker. Isaiah and Charlene West had sat him down one morning at breakfast and told him that pretty soon God was going to have a new home for him with permanent parents.

Jonas had come to love Isaiah and Charlene a lot. They didn't hurt him like his daddy had done, and he not only got used to Charlene's hugs and kisses, he needed them. He'd always known that his time with Isaiah and Charlene would be temporary, but he was still sad about leaving them.

As Jonas sat there at the fishing hole with Joe Baker, the man gently put his hand on his shoulder and asked, "Jonas, would you give Miss Betty and me a chance to be your momma and daddy?"

Suddenly, the little boy got a tug on his line and said

excitedly, "Look, Daddy, I got one. I got one." It was all Joe could do to keep himself from tearing up, because now he and Betty would finally have what they'd both yearned for: another child. Somehow Joe Baker knew that Early was rejoicing about all this.

CHAPTER EIGHTEEN

The Reverend Amos Booker found himself thinking more and more about Miss Mandy Johnson as he approached his twenty-sixth birthday. Amos knew how blessed he'd been by God, but he felt like there was still something missing. As he thought about Mandy's warm smile and her servant heart, he realized what was missing in his life—a godly wife! It was almost two years now since Wesley Johnson had passed, and Amos could tell that Mandy was ready to get on with the rest of her life. He'd so much enjoyed those moments of casual conversation with her at the House of Ribs, and that day at the picnic with her had been real special. Could Mandy Johnson possibly feel the same way about him? Amos Booker would know soon enough.

Mandy sat there on her coffee break at Kingsford's House of Ribs thinking about the Reverend Booker. The waitress job had been a real blessing for her after losing Wesley, but she knew that now the Lord was guiding her to get on with her life. She thought of all those friendly conversations she'd had with the young preacher when he'd come to the restaurant for a meal. What a godly—and yet down-to-earth man he seemed to be. And she remembered talking to Wesley shortly before he'd passed, and how he'd told her to rejoice if it turned out that God might someday have another husband for her. Mandy also knew that the congregation at Rock of Ages was praying for her, and she smiled as she thought of the joyous singing and praying at church and of the handsome young man in the pulpit. Could Amos possibly be attracted to her, she wondered? Miss Mandy Johnson would know soon enough.

CHAPTER NINETEEN

Kingsford's House of Ribs was all decorated up for the governor of Louisiana's visit. Charlene West, Betty Baker, and the other ladies at church had done a great job of making the restaurant look extra special, and now the excitement was growing as the governor's arrival got closer.

Isaiah West and his crew had prepared some awesome dishes for Governor and Mrs. Francois and their entourage: slow-cooked barbecue beef with spices, roasted potatoes, fresh mixed vegetables, iced coffee and sweet tea. For desert there was a huge, family-sized dish of peach and blackberry cobbler, with side servings of ice cream and hot fudge sauce.

Mandy Johnson had been selected to be one of the servers at the governor's table for this event, and she was honored—but not overcome. Whether it was a governor or a truck driver, she was still serving her Lord. Mandy was also happy because her uncle, Al Kingsford, had decided to turn over the opening luncheon prayer to Reverend Amos Booker. Though Mr. Al had always led the town in praying at community social events, for this special occasion he'd humbled himself and given the honor to the young preacher. To God be the Glory!

Amos Booker looked out over the assembled guests at the House of Ribs Restaurant—all gathered here for the governor's luncheon. He wanted to keep his prayer short because he knew that the governor was on a tight schedule. He also knew that Jules Francois couldn't wait to tear into the barbecue beef in front of him. Amos simply thanked God for the hands that prepared the food, welcomed the governor and Mrs. Francois and their staffs, and closed by asking the Lord's blessing on everyone at the House of Ribs. Then they all dug into an amazing spread of food and drinks.

Eddie Carlisle, the young supervisor from the Heavenly Angels Orphanage was sitting two tables over from the governor's table. Eddie had met with Mr. Al Kingsford a few days earlier and shown him the letter from his cousin at the State Capitol, confirming that Jules Francois wanted to talk to Eddie about the conditions at the orphanage when he visited the restaurant on his campaign stop.

Al was thrilled since he and others in the community had been praying about the horrors at Heavenly Angels for years. Eddie Carlisle's knock on his door was confirmation to Mr. Al Kingsford that God was about to intervene at the orphanage and to do a mighty work on behalf of the children there.

CHAPTER TWENTY

Amos Booker and Jonas Armstrong were sitting at the table next to Governor Francois. Amos could tell that Jules Francois and his wife, Helene, were well-pleased with the meal they'd been served. As Mandy Johnson and the other servers were clearing away the main course dishes and preparing to serve dessert, Amos's curiosity was aroused as he saw the governor and his wife dismiss their staff people and then invite a young stranger to their table. It was Eddie Carlisle. Amos and Jonas watched as Jules and Helene Francois had an animated conversation with Eddie.

Suddenly Al Kingsford appeared at the governor's side, bent over, and whispered something in his ear. The next thing Amos and Jonas knew they were being invited to sit down with the governor of Louisiana, his wife, and Eddie Carlisle. The day of reckoning had finally come for the director of the Heavenly Angels Orphanage, Master Roland.

The Reverend Amos Booker and Miss Mandy Johnson sat quietly in a booth sipping coffee at Kingsford's House of Ribs. Everyone else had left the governor's luncheon, and Amos and Mandy now had some time alone to relax and talk about the day's big event. Like all House of Ribs customers, Governor Francois had been won over by Mandy's warm smile and engaging manner as she waited on him and his people. And he shared with her that in his youth before politics he'd actually been a truck driver for awhile. Not only that, but Helene Francois told Mandy that she'd been a part-time waitress in her college days. The governor and his wife were just regular folks.

Then Amos told Mandy what had happened when he and Jonas were invited to sit at the governor's table. How he and Eddie Carlisle and Jonas Armstrong had spoken to Jules and Helene Francois about the true conditions at the Heavenly Angels Orphanage, and how the children were suffering there.

Helene Francois especially had looked shocked and then angry as she listened to their stories. Amos and Mandy both knew that something good was going to come out of this conversation with the governor. And they both knew as they reached across the booth and held hands, that the Lord was calling them into a very special ministry: the ministry of marriage.

CHAPTER TWENTY-ONE

Governor Jules Francois and his wife, Helene, were about to take a long-awaited vacation. After one term in office and a narrow election defeat, it was time to kick back and enjoy the good life. But first, there was one final matter to take care of: the Heavenly Angels Orphanage situation. Francois still couldn't get over what he'd heard from Eddie Carlisle, the Reverend Booker, and little Jonas Armstrong at the House of Ribs. He and Helene had sat there dumbfounded as Eddie and the others had filled them in on over twenty years of Master Roland's reign of terror at the orphanage. Jules Francois had been totally unaware of any of this. He'd been assured by his staff people and his other advisors that all was well in the state of Louisiana. No one had followed through for years on what the conditions really were at the Heavenly Angels Orphanage.

He didn't need for Helene to tell him that something had to be done. He already knew that. And shrewd politician that he was, he also knew that as he left office a great part of his legacy would be determined by how he responded to the damaging information he'd received about the orphanage. Francois gathered his public relations and spin control people together at the governor's mansion. A possible state scandal was about to be turned into a heroic farewell to Governor Jules Francois.

The headlines read: "Scandal Rocks Orphanage." All over the state of Louisiana the story was finally being told of the criminal and abusive activities that had been going on at the Heavenly Angels Orphanage for years. And the Six-O-Clock News led off with footage of Master Roland and his supervisors being handcuffed and placed in a state police van. Master Roland was defiant to the end—cursing at the crowd gathered outside the orphanage and trying to kick the state troopers as he was arrested. Most of his supervisors looked shaken and fearful as they were loaded into the van. There was also footage of the orphanage children—many of them looking surprised and bewildered at what was going on. Their day of deliverance had come at last, but it would take time for them to fully grasp all of this.

Heads were rolling at the state capitol as well. There was plenty of blame to go around. At his press conference, Governor Jules Francois gave a brief history of when the abuses had begun at Heavenly Angels and why they hadn't been discovered for years. Francois finished by praising three people: Eddie Carlisle, the Reverend Booker, and ten-year-old Jonas Armstrong. All of them were true Louisiana heroes. Then—on behalf of all the children at the orphanage—Governor Francois asked God's forgiveness for all the state administrators over the years that had neglected and not protected these orphans as they should have. A new day was dawning at the Heavenly Angels Orphanage as Jules Francois rode off into the sunset—his political legacy intact.

CHAPTER TWENTY-TWO

Amos Booker was a happy man. Eddie Carlisle was now an assistant to the new head of the Heavenly Angels Orphanage, a godly man named Benjamin Martin. Eddie and Mr. Martin wanted Amos and the folks at Rock of Ages Bible Church to set up a Sunday school program as well as regular chapel services for the children at Heavenly Angels. Volunteer teachers from the local schools would now be coming in to teach them reading, writing, and arithmetic. Sports, music, and other fun activities would also be on the agenda. Instead of a life of despair, these children would now have hope and opportunities—thanks to a great and merciful God.

Amos was also happy because little Jonas Armstrong was doing well in his new home with Joe and Betty Baker. The Lord had brought together a needy child with two people who wanted another chance at being parents, and He had blessed them all. The Reverend Amos Booker sat there quietly at the church parsonage content and joyous as he looked forward to the future—especially a future that would include Miss Mandy Johnson as his wife.

The Rock of Ages Bible Church was filled to

overflowing with family, friends, well-wishers, and honored guests: Jules and Helene Francois to celebrate the marriage of the Reverend Amos Booker and Miss Mandy Johnson. And everyone at the church knew that Reverend Waters, Early Baker, and Wesley Johnson were rejoicing in Heaven over this happy day.

The preacher from another nearby church, the Reverend Willie Rice, would be officiating. The Rock of Ages choir had prepared some special old-time gospel music—complete with joyous singing, clapping, and even a little dancing. As Mr. Al Kingsford walked his niece, Mandy, down the aisle, there were applause and cries of "Hallelujah" and Praise God from the congregation. Isaiah West and Amos waited for them at the altar. Amos saw the joy in his momma Charlene's eyes, and he blew her a kiss and then touched his heart. Words weren't needed. The Reverend Amos Booker and his new wife, Mandy, were now ready for the next chapter in their lives.

Thomas Rhodes is a freelance writer and small business operator living in New Hampshire.